The
Perfect Place
for a Picnic

by Katie Dale and Rory Walker

W

It was a lovely sunny day.

"Let's go for a picnic," said Mo.

"Good idea," said Yaz.

Mo put a big red rug into a basket.

Then he packed a fizzy drink

and some sandwiches.

Yaz packed apples and some crisps.

"Yum!" said Mo. "This is

a perfect picnic!"

"Let's find

the perfect place

for the picnic,"

said Yaz.

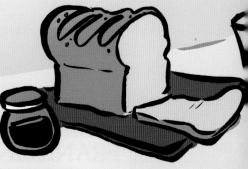

Mo and Yaz went to the park.
Yaz put the big red rug down
on the grass and got out
the fizzy drink.
"This is the perfect place
for a picnic," she said.
But ...

"Oh no!" said Mo.

"The grass is wet!"

Mo and Yaz went to the beach.
Mo put the rug down on the sand
and opened the crisps. "This is
the perfect place for a picnic,"
he said. But ...

"Oh no!" cried Mo.

"The sand has got in the crisps!"

Mo and Yaz got into a boat.

"This is the perfect place

for a picnic," Yaz said.

Mo unpacked the basket. But ...

"Oh no!" said Mo.

"The seagull has taken
our sandwiches!"

Mo and Yaz went to the farm.

They sat on the big red rug

on a wall in the sun.

"This is the perfect place

for a picnic," Mo said.

But ...

"Oh no!" said Mo.

"I can see an angry bull! Run!"

Mo and Yaz went to a forest.
Yaz put the rug on a little hill and
poured the fizzy drink.
"This is the perfect place
for a picnic," she said. But ...

"Oh NO!" shouted Mo and Yaz.

"It's an anthill!"

"Where can we go for our picnic?"
said Yaz.

"I know!" said Mo. "Follow me."

Yaz and Mo sat on their big red rug.

"This is the perfect place
for a picnic," said Mo.

"Yes. Just perfect," laughed Yaz.

Story order

Look at these 5 pictures and captions.
Put the pictures in the right order
to retell the story.

1

Mo and Yaz go to the farm.

2

Mo and Yaz pack a picnic.

3

A seagull steals some food.

4

The wind sends sand flying.

5

Mo and Yaz make a new picnic at home.

Independent Reading

This series is designed to provide an opportunity for your child to read on their own. These notes are written for you to help your child choose a book and to read it independently.

In school, your child's teacher will often be using reading books which have been banded to support the process of learning to read. Use the book band colour your child is reading in school to help you make a good choice. *The Perfect Place for a Picnic* is a good choice for children reading at Orange Band in their classroom to read independently. The aim of independent reading is to read this book with ease, so that your child enjoys the story and relates it to their own experiences.

About the book

It's the perfect weather for a picnic, but Mo and Yaz keep running into problems as they try to find the perfect place for their picnic.

Before reading

Help your child to learn how to make good choices by asking: "Why did you choose this book? Why do you think you will enjoy it?" Look at the cover together and ask: "What do you think the story will be about?" Ask your child to think of what they already know about the story context. Then ask your child to read the title aloud. Establish that in this book, two children will go on a picnic.

Ask: "What do you know about picnics outside? What places do you like to have a picnic?"

Remind your child that they can sound out the letters to make a word if they get stuck.

Decide together whether your child will read the story independently or read it aloud to you.

During reading

Remind your child of what they know and what they can do independently. If reading aloud, support your child if they hesitate or ask for help by telling the word. If reading to themselves, remind your child that they can come and ask for your help if stuck.

After reading

Support comprehension by asking your child to tell you about the story. Use the story order puzzle to encourage your child to retell the story in the right sequence, in their own words. The correct sequence can be found at the bottom of the next page.

Help your child think about the messages in the book that go beyond the story and ask: "How do you feel when things go wrong? Do you give up or try to find a new idea?"

Give your child a chance to respond to the story: "Did you have a favourite part? Which scene was the funniest? The most surprising? Why?"

Extending learning

Help your child understand the story structure by using the same sentence patterning and adding different elements. "Let's make up a new story about having a picnic. Where will your picnic take place? What might go wrong at the picnic? How can the picnickers solve the problem?"

In the classroom, your child's teacher may be teaching adding the suffix -ed to the end of verbs, to make the simple past tense.

There are examples in this book that you could look at with your child, for example: *packed, unpacked, started, laughed.*

Franklin Watts
First published in Great Britain in 2020
by The Watts Publishing Group

Series Editors: Jackie Hamley, Melanie Palmer and Grace Glendinning
Series Advisors: Dr Sue Bodman and Glen Franklin
Series Designer: Peter Scoulding and Cathryn Gilbert

A CIP catalogue record for this book is
available from the British Library.

ISBN 978 1 4451 7102 9 (hbk)
ISBN 978 1 4451 7100 5 (pbk)
ISBN 978 1 4451 7101 2 (library ebook)

Printed in China

Franklin Watts
An imprint of
Hachette Children's Group
Part of The Watts Publishing Group
Carmelite House
50 Victoria Embankment
London EC4Y 0DZ

An Hachette UK Company
www.hachette.co.uk

www.franklinwatts.co.uk

Answer to Story order: 2, 4, 3, 1, 5